ONE HUNDRED PERCENT ME

Renee Macalino Rutledge

Illustrated by Anita Prades

BLOOM BOOKS
FOR YOUNG READERS

Published by:
Bloom Books for Young Readers,
an imprint of Ulysses Press
PO Box 3440
Berkeley, CA 94703
www.ulyssespress.com

ISBN: 978-1-64604-348-4

Printed in China
10 9 8 7 6 5 4 3 2 1

Acquisitions editor: Claire Sielaff
Managing editor: Claire Chun
Copyeditor: Julie Holland
Proofreader: Joyce Wu
Cover design: Jake Flaherty

This product conforms to all applicable CPSC and CPSIA standards
Source of production: Prosperous Printing, Shenzhen, Guangdong, China
Date of production: December 2021
Production run: PP202112-1

For Chris, Maya, Raina,
and our extended family.

For the ancestors who came before
and the descendants who will follow.

Mama, Papi, and I walked our dog around the block. We passed a neighbor watering the flowers in his garden. He stopped to chat.

"Wow, you look just like your mom and dad!" he told me. "Fifty-fifty."

I looked up at my parents and imagined half of my face like Mama's, half like Papi's. That didn't seem right.

4

"Do you think I look exactly like you?" I asked them.

"You may take after us, our parents, and their parents in many ways," Papi said. "But that makes you different from all of us."

"You look like yourself," Mama replied.

I agreed. "I'm one hundred percent me."

That Saturday, Mama, Papi, and I rode the BART train to the 16th Street station. We were on our way to the Mission District, where hundreds of colorful murals make the neighborhood come to life.

"Where are you from?" a lady wearing a green coat asked me.

I thought about Oakland, where I live and grew up. On Saturdays, we like to walk around Oakland and visit different neighborhoods. We go to Lake Merritt. Then we buy dim sum in Chinatown or kimchee soup in Koreatown for dinner. On Sundays, we like to go to the artisan market in Jack London Square.

"I'm from Oakland," I replied.

The lady with the green coat
squinted, then shook her head.

"I mean, where is your family
from?" she asked.

This made me think of Papi and Mama, and my grandparents, too.

Papi is from New York. His parents are from Puerto Rico.

Mama is from San Francisco. Her parents are from the Philippines.

"My family is from New York, Puerto Rico, San Francisco, and the Philippines," I replied. "I'm from Oakland, and I'm one hundred percent me."

"That you are!" the lady with the green coat said. At the next stop, she tipped her hat before stepping off the train.

After seeing the murals, we went to Abuela's house for *arroz con pollo*. My *tío* and *tía*, or aunt and uncle, were there, too. We sat together around the kitchen table.

"You are growing up so fast," my tío exclaimed. "You have your papi's eyes!"

"Yes, she does," my tía agreed. "*Qué linda*, how pretty! You take after your Latina side."

When I didn't reply, my tío asked, "Aren't you proud to have your papi's eyes?"

I'm proud to look like my papi, but my eyes are not his eyes. My eyes belong to me. Now I knew what to say.

"My eyes are a little like my papi's and a little like my mama's. They are my own, and I'm one hundred percent me!"

My tío laughed from deep in his belly, and my tía squeezed my arm lovingly.

"*Seguro*, you absolutely are," they agreed.
They each gave me a high five.

The next day, at the artisan market, I admired the pretty beanies while Mama looked for a pair of beaded shell earrings at the booth next door.

"I like this one," I told Mama, pointing to a woven purple beanie with a pink peace sign in the middle.

The lady in the booth rang
us up and said, "I'm sorry if
I've been staring. You have
such an interesting face.
May I ask, what are you?"

She took another long look
at me.

Mama knew what she meant.

"She's mixed," Mama replied. "I'm Asian, and her dad's Latino."

The lady in the booth nodded.

Mama answers this question about me all the time. But I had an answer, too.

"My family is from New York, Puerto Rico, San Francisco, and the Philippines," I said. "I'm from Oakland. My eyes are my own. I'm mixed, and I'm one hundred percent me!"

"How wonderful!" the lady in the booth exclaimed, with her hand on her heart. She threw a button with a picture of the Earth into my bag, free of charge, to pin on my new beanie.

At the sound of the recess bell at school on Monday, I raced to the monkey bars with my good friends Imani and Perla.

A boy in our class came over and said, "You look like sisters. Are you sisters?"

Imani's family is from Oakland, India, and Kenya.

Perla and her parents are from Los Angeles, and her grandparents are from Mexico.

"We are not sisters," Imani said.

"We are ourselves," Perla added.

"Just like you," I answered.

Imani, Perla, and I linked arms and skipped to the swings. We swung high, together.

The next weekend, I sat with my *lolo* and *lola*, *tita* and *tito*—
my mama's parents, sister, and brother-in-law—at my cousin's
softball game.

In between cheering, they spent part of the game talking
about me.

"She looks more Filipina than Puerto Rican," my tita said.

"I disagree. She is growing up to look more and more like her dad," my tito said.

"She reminds me so much of my own lola," my lola said. "My grandmother was a mestiza, too."

"What do you think?" my lolo asked me.

Before replying, I thought about the questions that the lady with the green coat, my tío and my tía, the lady in the booth, and the boy from school had asked. I knew what I wanted to say.

"My face has some of my dad, some of my mom, and even some of my great-great-grandmother. My face is not like anyone else's, and I'm one hundred percent me," I said.

"Well said!" my tito exclaimed, smiling.

"Home run!" cheered my tita, and I knew she wasn't talking about softball.

That night, my parents called me to the living room. They each had a piece of paper to show me. The papers showed some test results. But they were not from the type of tests I take at school.

"We've had our DNA tested," Mama said. She explained that DNA are spiral-shaped instruction books for the cells in our bodies. The information in the spirals helps decide the color of our eyes and hair, our height, and even the shape and size of our noses.

"These test results also help us to learn more about our ancestry, or the people we are related to, even from a long time ago," Papi added.

The DNA test results showed Papi's ancestors come not just from Puerto Rico, but also from Italy, Spain, Portugal, France, and Nigeria and Northern Africa. He has Indigenous Puerto Rican ancestry, too.

Mama's ancestors come not just from the Philippines, but also from China and Spain.

I learned that my ancestors grew up in many different parts of the world.

Mama, Papi, and I agreed that we are all unique, but connected.

That makes me feel a little bit closer to everyone, even people I'm not related to. Whether we know our ancestors or not, we all have them.

"They are like the roots of a sacred and beautiful tree, and we are like the branches," Mama said.

I could have my own DNA ancestry test done if I wanted to, Mama and Papi told me. Maybe I will someday. But for now, it is enough for me to know:

My family is from New York, Puerto Rico, San Francisco, and the Philippines.

I am from Oakland.

My eyes are my own.

I'm mixed.

My face is not like anyone else's.

My ancestors grew up in many different parts of the world.

We are all unique, but connected.

And most of all…

I am one hundred percent me!

About the Author

Renee Macalino Rutledge was born in Manila, Philippines, and raised in California from the age of four. Her debut novel, *The Hour of Daydreams*, won an Institute for Immigration Research New American Voices Finalist award, Foreword INDIES Gold, and Powell's Top Five Staff Pick. In addition to *One Hundred Percent Me*, she is also the author of the children's book *Buckley the Highland Cow & Ralphy the Goat*, a story about overcoming hardship with the help of friends who are often very different from ourselves. Renee lives in the San Francisco Bay Area, where she reads books for a living, loves the outdoors, and is always on the lookout for a new adventure with her husband and their two daughters. Find her at www.reneerutledge.com or connect with her on Instagram @renee_rutledge.

About the Illustrator

Anita Prades is an illustrator and actress born and based in São Paulo, Brazil. She graduated with a visual arts degree from UNESP (Universidade Estadual "Júlio de Mesquita Filho") and holds a master's degree in arts and education from the same institution. She has illustrated several children's books in Brazil, with titles selected for the Brazilian Catalogue of Bologna Children's Book Fair in 2015 and 2017. In 2020, Anita published her first book as an author, *Fio de Rio* (*River Thread*), and she has been working on new books and personal projects ever since. *One Hundred Percent Me* is her first international experience as an illustrator. Anita is also a team member of Instituto Emília (emilia.org.br), an independent and free digital publication with international recognition dedicated to children's literature and the formation of young readers. Find her at www.anitaprades.com.